Roberta
and Me

Sibylle & Jürgen Rieckhoff

Translated by Vera Müller

FRANCES LINCOLN CHILDREN'S BOOKS

It was love at first sight.

When I met Roberta for the first time,
I knew straight away that we belonged together.
I crept up to her to say hello and she didn't
run away like a silly scaredy-sheep. She was
brave and dignified and just the sheep for me.

I've always wanted a pet. I did have a dog
who adopted me once. Well, maybe not adopted
exactly – I had to give him a bit of encouragement.
But you're not allowed to do that and I had
to give him back to his owner.

I could have had one of Michaela's cat's kittens,
but I couldn't decide which one I wanted and Mum
didn't want seven.

Roberta, on the other hand, was all by herself,
and that was perfect.

"Isn't she rather big?" asked Mum. She had imagined
something a bit smaller and easier to keep.

   Dad wasn't all that keen either. But I can be
very persuasive when I really want something
and in the end, they gave in.

Baah!

"Are you sure she wants to come with you?"
said Dad.

So I asked her, "Roberta, would you like
to come with us?"

Roberta stood there, looking around
and chewing. "BAAAAH!" she said.

So then we just had to ask the farmer.
He had so many sheep he wouldn't miss one,
would he? But we decided to check.

"All right," growled the farmer, "take her.
I don't mind."
   Roberta was ours!

Life was a bit difficult at first. After all, Roberta came
from the countryside and the city was new to her.
There were some things she just couldn't understand.
But I was sure that with a lot of love and patience
she would get used to city life.

We had to make new rules in our flat
and decide where Roberta was going to live.
 Mum bought her a sheepskin blanket
and put it in the hall, but Roberta didn't like that.
She was a friendly sheep and wanted to be with
the family - and when she made up her mind
about something, it was hard to shift her.

Mealtimes were interesting. Roberta was a strict vegetarian but she didn't mind that we weren't. She just wanted to eat at the table with us.

We had lots of visitors because everyone wanted to meet Roberta. And they all liked her very much. There was only one problem...

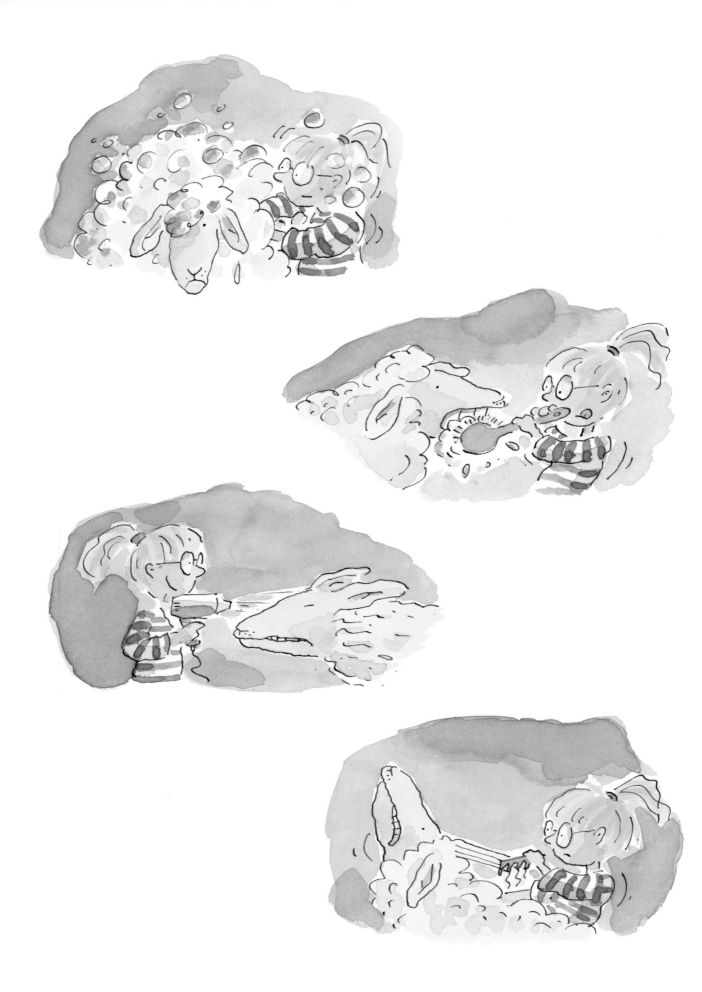

The smell. It wasn't all that strong, but Mum
was right, it was certainly noticeable. We tried
opening the windows, but in the end we all agreed –
Roberta needed some grooming. That was
the only time she was really grumpy. I don't think
she liked her lemon-scented fleece at all.

When we went for walks, Roberta caused a bit
of a stir. I was proud of her, but she took it all
in her stride. Soon the whole street knew us
and Roberta could have had lots of friends.
But she was quite choosy and I must admit
I was glad. I was her special friend.

While I was at school Roberta had to spend
the day at home. But she was bored, and sometimes
she did silly things, so Mum started taking Roberta
with her to the supermarket.

Roberta and I had a great time. She was cuddly
and snuggly, we enjoyed each other's company
and never disagreed. But sometimes Roberta
seemed to be longing for something. And I started
to wonder if she was really happy.

So we went on a trip to the countryside.

    Roberta's eyes began to shine as soon as we left
the city. When she saw all the other sheep her little
tail wagged with joy.

    I knew then that our time together was over.
I kissed Roberta goodbye.

Mum and Dad gave me Robert to stop
me being too sad. Robert's quite nice,
I suppose. He doesn't need much room
and he's made of cotton so I can put him
in the washing machine when he starts
to smell.

But one day I am sure…

I will get another pet!